何 不 浅 尝 辄 止
joy of first glimpse

浅尝诗丛

雏菊轻柔地追随太阳

浪漫花语诗

·中英双语·

江苏凤凰文艺出版社
JIANGSU PHOENIX LITERATURE AND
ART PUBLISHING

[美]艾米莉·狄金森 等 著
凤凰诗歌出版中心 编　程旗 译

图书在版编目（CIP）数据

雏菊轻柔地追随太阳：浪漫花语诗/（美）艾米莉·狄金森等著；程旗译. ——南京：江苏凤凰文艺出版社，2023.9

（浅尝诗丛）

ISBN 978-7-5594-7911-2

Ⅰ.①雏… Ⅱ.①艾…②程… Ⅲ.①诗集-美国-现代 Ⅳ.①I712.25

中国国家版本馆CIP数据核字(2023)第157399号

雏菊轻柔地追随太阳：浪漫花语诗

(美)艾米莉·狄金森等 著 程 旗 译

出 版 人	张在健
责任编辑	王娱瑶 徐 辰
装帧设计	徐芳芳
责任印制	刘 巍
出版发行	江苏凤凰文艺出版社
	南京市中央路165号，邮编：210009
出版社网址	http://www.jswenyi.com
印 刷	江苏凤凰新华印务集团有限公司
开 本	880毫米×1230毫米 1/32
印 张	7
字 数	110千字
版 次	2023年9月第1版 2023年9月第1次印刷
标准书号	ISBN 978-7-5594-7911-2
定 价	42.00元

江苏凤凰文艺版图书凡印刷、装订错误，可向出版社调换，联系电话 025-83280257

CONTENT

目录

Rose
玫瑰

002　A Red, Red Rose (Robert Burns)
003　一朵红红的玫瑰（罗伯特·彭斯）

004　Sea Rose (Hilda Doolittle)
005　海玫瑰（希尔达·杜利特尔）

006　Blue Roses (Rudyard Kipling)
007　蓝玫瑰（鲁德亚德·吉卜林）

008　Nobody Knows This Little Rose (Emily Dickinson)
009　无人识此小蔷薇（艾米莉·狄金森）

010　Roses (George Eliot)
011　玫瑰（乔治·艾略特）

012 The Sick Rose (William Blake)
013 病玫瑰（威廉·布莱克）

014 Red Roses (Langston Hughes)
015 红玫瑰（兰斯顿·休斯）

016 My Pretty Rose Tree (William Blake)
017 我美丽的玫瑰树（威廉·布莱克）

018 A Sepal, Petal, and a Thorn (Emily Dickinson)
019 一片花萼，一枚花瓣，和一根花刺（艾米莉·狄金森）

020 A Little Budding Rose (Emily Bronte)
021 一朵含苞待放的小玫瑰（艾米莉·勃朗特）

022 The Rose (Sara Teasdale)
023 玫瑰（萨拉·提斯黛尔）

024 Song of The Rose (Edith Nesbit)
025 玫瑰之歌（伊迪丝·内斯比特）

Daffodil
水仙

028 I Wandered Lonely as a Cloud (William Wordsworth)
030 我孤独地漫步,像一朵流云(威廉·华兹华斯)

032 To an Early Daffodil (Amy Lowell)
033 致早萌的水仙(艾米·洛威尔)

034 Daffodil Time (Clinton Scollard)
036 水仙时光(克林顿·斯科拉德)

038 In Time of Daffodils (Edward Estlin Cummings)
039 在水仙花的时节(爱德华·埃斯特林·卡明斯)

040 Daffodil Dawn (Olive Eleanor Custance)
041 黄水仙黎明(奥列佛·艾莉诺·卡斯坦斯)

042 Where Ships of Purple—Gently Toss (Emily Dickinson)
043 紫色的船儿轻轻摇(艾米莉·狄金森)

Tulip
郁金香

046 A Tulip Garden (Amy Lowell)
047 郁金香花园（艾米·洛威尔）

048 The Tulip Bed (William Carlos Williams)
050 郁金香花圃（威廉·卡洛斯·威廉姆斯）

052 Hora Stellatrix (Amy Lowell)
053 霍拉·史黛拉翠克斯（艾米·洛威尔）

054 Bulb Planting Time (Edgar Albert Guest)
056 球茎种植时间（埃德加·阿尔伯特·盖思特）

058 To A Tulip-Bulb (Edith Nesbit)
060 致郁金香球茎（伊迪丝·内斯比特）

062 Leaves (Amelie Rives)
063 叶（艾蜜莉·莱夫斯）

Violet
紫罗兰

066　Sweet Violets (Dorothy Parker)
067　甜美的紫罗兰（多萝西·帕克）

068　Autumn Violets (Christina Rossetti)
069　秋日的紫罗兰（克里斯蒂娜·罗塞蒂）

070　The Violet (Jane Taylor)
071　紫罗兰（珍·泰勒）

072　The Yellow Violet (William Cullen Bryant)
074　黄色紫罗兰（威廉·卡伦·布莱恩特）

076　Wood Violets (Kate Brownlee Sherwood)
079　林地紫罗兰（凯特·布朗利·舍伍德）

Iris
鸢尾

084　Flame.Yellow-Iris (Frances Sargent Osgood)
085　火焰.黄色鸢尾花（弗朗西斯·萨金特·奥斯古德）

086　Sea Iris (Hilda Doolittle)
088　海鸢尾（希尔达·杜利特尔）

090　Poppy Seed—In a Garden (Amy Lowell)
092　罂粟种子——在花园里（艾米·洛威尔）

094　The France Flower (John Galsworthy)
095　法国之花（约翰·高尔斯华绥）

096　Iris (Louise Driscoll)
097　鸢尾花（露易丝·德里斯科尔）

098　On Such a Day (Mary Elizabeth Coleridge)
099　在这样的日子里（玛丽·伊丽莎白·柯勒律治）

100　Not Iris in Her Pride (George Peele)
101　矜傲的鸢尾花不会……（乔治·皮尔）

103　Scent of Irises (David Herbert Lawrence)
106　鸢尾花香（戴维·赫伯特·劳伦斯）

Lilac
紫丁香

110 When Lilacs Last in the Dooryard Bloomed (Walt Whitman)
111 当紫丁香最后一次在庭院开放（沃尔特·惠特曼）

112 The Lilac (Humbert Wolfe)
113 紫丁香（亨伯特·沃尔夫）

114 A Song of the Lilac (Louise Imogen Guiney)
115 紫丁香之歌（露易丝·伊莫金·吉尼）

116 Somebody Brought in Lilac (Lesbia Harford)
117 有人送来了丁香花（莱斯比亚·哈福德）

Orchid
兰花

120 At Baia (Hilda Doolittle)
122 在巴亚（希尔达·杜利特尔）

124 Orchids (Theodore Wratislaw)
126 兰花（西奥多·拉蒂斯劳）

Jasmine
茉莉花

130 Jasmines (Claude McKay)
131 茉莉花（克劳德·麦凯）

132 The First Jasmines (Rabindranath Tagore)
134 第一次的茉莉（罗宾德拉纳特·泰戈尔）

Lily
百合

136 The Lily (William Blake)
137 百合花（威廉·布莱克）

138 The Lily and the Bee (Henry Lawson)
140 百合与蜜蜂（亨利·劳森）

142 A Lyric to Lily (Charles Henry Webb)
144 献给百合的抒情诗（查尔斯·亨利·韦伯）

146 Loneliness (Danske Bedinger Dandridge)
148 孤独（丹斯克·贝丁格·丹德里奇）

Waterlily
莲花

150 Water Lilies (Sara Teasdale)
151 睡莲（萨拉·提斯黛尔）

152 Water Lily (Rainer Maria Rilke)
153 睡莲（莱纳·玛利亚·里尔克）

154 The Lotus (Rabindranath Tagore)
155 莲花（罗宾德拉纳特·泰戈尔）

Daisy
雏菊

158 So Has A Daisy Vanished (Emily Dickinson)
159 一朵雏菊就这样消失（艾米莉·狄金森）

160 The Daisy Follows Soft the Sun (Emily Dickinson)
161 雏菊轻柔地追随太阳（艾米莉·狄金森）

162 Daisy Time (Marjorie Pickthall)
163 雏菊时节（玛乔丽·皮克索尔）

164 Little Daisy (Jurgis Baltrušaitis)
165 小雏菊（尤吉斯·巴楚萨蒂斯）

Rosemary
迷迭香

168 Rosemary (Edna St. Vincent Millay)
169 迷迭香（埃德娜·圣·文森特·米莱）

170 To Rosemary (Stephen Vincent Benet)
172 致迷迭香（史蒂芬·文森特·贝内特）

174 Rosemary (Marianne Moore)
176 迷迭香（玛丽安·摩尔）

178 Rosemary (Ernest McGaffey)
179 迷迭香（欧内斯特·麦加菲）

Others
其他

182 The Easter Flower (Claude McKay)
183 复活节之花（克劳德·麦凯）

184 Wind and Window Flower (Robert Frost)
186 风与窗花（罗伯特·弗罗斯特）

188 Rose Pogonias (Robert Frost)
190 玫瑰朱兰（罗伯特·弗罗斯特）

192 Blue Squills (Sara Teasdale)
193 蓝铃花（萨拉·提斯黛尔）

194 As If Some Little Arctic Flower (Emily Dickinson)
195 如同一朵北极的小花（艾米莉·狄金森）

196 Ah! Sun-Flower (William Blake)
197 啊，向阳花（威廉·布莱克）

198 Flowers (Thomas Hood)
200 花（托马斯·胡德）

202 Pear Tree (Hilda Doolittle)
203 梨树（希尔达·杜利特尔）

Rose
玫瑰

A Red, Red Rose

by Robert Burns

O, my Luve's like a red, red rose,
That's newly sprung in June.
O, my Luve's like the melodie,
That's sweetly play'd in tune.

As fair art thou, my bonnie lass,
So deep in luve am I,
And I will luve thee still, my dear,
Till a' the seas gang dry!

Till a' the seas gang dry, my dear,
And the rocks melt wi' the sun!
And I will luve thee still, my dear,
While the sands o' life shall run.

And fare thee weel, my only Luve!
And fare thee weel, a while!
And I will come again, my Luve,
Tho' it were ten thousand mile!

一朵红红的玫瑰

[英国] 罗伯特·彭斯

哦，我的爱人像红红的玫瑰，
在六月里新鲜初放。
哦，我的爱人如曼妙的乐曲，
悦耳的音调甜蜜奏响。

你如此美丽，我心爱的姑娘，
我对你情深似海，
对你的爱永不更改，我亲爱的，
直到那海水全部枯竭！

直到那海水全部枯竭，我亲爱的，
直到岩石被日晒熔化！
对你的爱永不更改，我亲爱的，
只要生命的沙漏尚未停歇。

别了，我唯一的爱人！
让我们暂且别离！
我还会回来，我的爱人，
哪怕是千里万里！

Sea Rose

by Hilda Doolittle

Rose, harsh rose,

marred and with stint of petals,

meagre flower, thin,

sparse of leaf,

more precious

than a wet rose

single on a stem—

you are caught in the drift.

Stunted, with small leaf,

you are flung on the sand,

you are lifted

in the crisp sand

that drives in the wind.

Can the spice-rose

drip such acrid fragrance

hardened in a leaf?

海玫瑰

[美国] 希尔达·杜利特尔

玫瑰,粗粝的玫瑰,
玷污折损,花瓣零落,
花朵羸弱单薄,
花叶稀疏,

比独立枝头的
淋湿的玫瑰
更为珍贵——
你被水流卷起。

发育不良、叶片细小,
你被抛掷于沙滩上,
细碎干燥的沙粒
将你裹挟举起,
随风驱驰飘荡。

那芬芳的玫瑰
如何能散发　凝固在一片叶中的
犀利香气?

Blue Roses

by Rudyard Kipling

Roses red and roses white,
Plucked I for my love's delight.
She would none of all my posies—
Bade me gather her blue roses.

Half the world I wandered through,
Seeking where such flowers grew.
Half the world unto my quest,
Answered me with laugh and jest.

Home I came at wintertide,
But my silly love had died,
Seeking with her latest breath,
Roses from the arms of Death.

It may be beyond the grave,
She shall find what she would have.
Mine was but an idle quest—
Roses white and red are best!

蓝玫瑰

[英国] 鲁德亚德·吉卜林

玫瑰红,玫瑰白,
为取悦爱人,我特意采摘。
可所有花束,她都不屑一顾——
要我为她采来 蓝色的玫瑰。

我游荡漂泊了半个世界,
遍寻这花朵生长之处。
我四处索问的回报
是半个世界的讥讽嘲笑。

寒冬时节我才归家,
而愚蠢的爱人已香消玉殒。
她用最后的一息,
从死神的臂弯把玫瑰找寻。

或许只有在坟茔之外,
她才能找到自己所爱。
我的探求不过是徒劳——
最美的玫瑰,就是红与白!

Nobody Knows This Little Rose

by Emily Dickinson

Nobody knows this little Rose—

It might a pilgrim be

Did I not take it from the ways

And lift it up to thee.

Only a Bee will miss it—

Only a Butterfly,

Hastening from far journey—

On its breast to lie—

Only a Bird will wonder—

Only a Breeze will sigh—

Ah Little Rose—how easy

For such as thee to die!

无人识此小蔷薇

[美国] 艾米莉·狄金森

无人识此小蔷薇——

若非我把它从路旁摘下,

举来献你,

它还像个流浪者,独自孤寂。

只有一只蜜蜂会把它想起——

只有一只蝴蝶

从遥远的旅途匆匆飞落——

在它的胸脯驻足停歇——

只有小鸟为它惊奇——

只有微风为它叹息——

啊,这小小的蔷薇——多么容易

像你一样凋零逝去!

Roses

by George Eliot

You love the roses—so do I. I wish
The sky would rain down roses, as they rain
From off the shaken bush. Why will it not?
Then all the valley would be pink and white
And soft to tread on. They would fall as light
As feathers, smelling sweet; and it would be
Like sleeping and like waking, all at once!

玫瑰

[英国] 乔治·艾略特

你爱玫瑰——我也一样。我希望
天空能落下玫瑰花雨,花瓣纷落如雨
从摇曳的灌木枝头飘洒。为什么不呢?
粉红雪白,将铺满整个山谷,
脚底绵软。若是在上面漫步,
花瓣飘落,芬芳扑鼻,如羽毛般轻盈;
这美妙的花境,如梦,似醒!

The Sick Rose

by William Blake

O Rose thou art sick.

The invisible worm,

That flies in the night

In the howling storm:

Has found out thy bed

Of crimson joy:

And his dark secret love

Does thy life destroy.

病玫瑰

[英国] 威廉·布莱克

哦,玫瑰,你病了。
隐秘无形的蠕虫,
趁那夜色飞来,
伴着风暴呼啸:

栖上你这处花床,
安享这绯红的欢悦:
他黑暗隐秘的爱情,
摧毁了 你的生命。

Red Roses

by Langston Hughes

I'm waitin' for de springtime
When de tulips grow—
Sweet, sweet springtime
When de tulips grow;
Cause if I'd die in de winter
They'd bury me under snow.

Un'neath de snow, Lawd,
Oh, what would I do?
Un'neath de snow,
I say what would I do?
It's bad enough to die but
I don't want freezin' too.

I'm waitin' for de springtime
An' de roses red,
Waitin' for de springtime
When de roses red.
'Ll make a nice coverin'
Fer a gal that's dead.

红玫瑰

[美国] 兰斯顿·休斯

我在等待春日时光,
彼时有郁金香生长——
芬芳甜蜜的春日时光,
有郁金香葱郁生长;
因为我若在冬季死去,
他们将把我埋葬于雪里。

在冰雪之下,上帝呀,
我可怎么度日?
被冰雪遮覆,
我该如何自处?
死亡已足够糟糕,
我不愿再受冰冻煎熬。

我在等待春日时光,
彼时玫瑰嫣红绽放,
待到春日时光,
玫瑰嫣红绽放。
那将是面绝美的罩纱,
献给一位死去的姑娘。

My Pretty Rose Tree

by William Blake

A flower was offered to me,
Such a flower as May never bore;
But I said "I've a pretty rose tree",
And I passed the sweet flower o'er.

Then I went to my pretty rose tree,
To tend her by day and by night.
But my rose turned away with jealousy,
And her thorns were my only delight.

我美丽的玫瑰树

[英国] 威廉·布莱克

有人送我鲜花一枝,
它美得不像五月的风物;
但我说"我有棵美丽的玫瑰树",
便将那娇美的花弃掷不顾。

我走向我美丽的玫瑰树,
精心照拂,夜以继日。
可我的玫瑰心怀嫉妒、转脸拒绝,
只剩她的尖刺,予我喜悦慰藉。

A Sepal, Petal, and a Thorn

by Emily Dickinson

A sepal, petal, and a thorn

Upon a common summer's morn—

A flask of Dew—A Bee or two—

A Breeze—a caper in the trees—

And I'm a Rose!

一片花萼,一枚花瓣,和一根花刺

[美国]艾米莉·狄金森

一片花萼,一枚花瓣,和一根花刺

在一个寻常的夏日黎明——

一瓶露水——一两只蜜蜂——

一缕清风——一阵林间的欢跃——

而我,是一枝蔷薇!

A Little Budding Rose

by Emily Bronte

It was a little budding rose,
Round like a fairy globe,
And shyly did its leaves unclose
Hid in their mossy robe,
But sweet was the slight and spicy smell
It breathed from its heart invisible.

The rose is blasted, withered, blighted,
Its root has felt a worm,
And like a heart beloved and slighted,
Failed, faded, shrunk its form.
Bud of beauty, bonnie flower,
I stole thee from thy natal bower.

I was the worm that withered thee,
Thy tears of dew all fell for me;
Leaf and stalk and rose are gone,
Exile earth they died upon.

Yes, that last breath of balmy scent
With alien breezes sadly blent!

一朵含苞待放的小玫瑰

[英国]艾米莉·勃朗特

这是朵含苞待放的小玫瑰,
圆润得像颗仙女球,
它羞怯舒展的叶片
隐匿在苔藓礼袍下面,
它心底的呼吸,隐不可见
却细微刺激、芬芳甜蜜。

这株玫瑰饱受摧残、凋萎创伤,
它的根部有蠕虫滋长,
如一颗心,先被深爱、又受冷落,
便失意、减色、形容消瘦。
美丽的蓓蕾,娇媚的花朵,
我把你从故园的阴凉处偷走。

我就是那让你枯萎的蠕虫,
你的露珠泪水为我流淌;
茎、叶与花都已败落,
在放逐之地仙逝消亡。

哦,异乡的微风
将最后的温香气息,凄婉吹送!

The Rose

by Sara Teasdale

Beneath my chamber window

Pierrot was singing, singing;

I heard his lute the whole night thru

Until the east was red.

Alas, alas Pierrot,

I had no rose for flinging

Save one that drank my tears for dew

Before its leaves were dead.

I found it in the darkness,

I kissed it once and threw it,

The petals scattered over him,

His song was turned to joy;

And he will never know—

Alas, the one who knew it!

The rose was plucked when dusk was dim

Beside a laughing boy.

玫瑰

[美国] 萨拉·提斯黛尔

在我卧室的窗户下面
皮埃罗在唱呀唱;
我整晚都听到他的琴音
直到东方吐露红光。
哎呀呀,皮埃罗,
我没有其他玫瑰可以投掷
唯有一支,叶子濒临枯死
啜饮我的眼泪作为露汁。

我在黑暗中找寻到它,
亲吻一下,又把它丢弃,
花瓣洒落在他身上,
他的歌声转忧为喜;
哎,他永远不会懂得
了解这枝花的人!
玫瑰被折断时,暮色昏暗,
而它旁边的男孩,笑容满面。

注:pierrot(皮埃罗),意大利喜剧中的丑角形象,常在文学作品中作为悲伤的小丑,象征爱情和孤独。

Song of The Rose
by Edith Nesbit

THE lilac-time is over,
Laburnum's day is past,
The red may-blossoms cover
The white ones, fallen too fast.
And guelder-roses hang like snow,
Where purple flag-flowers grow.

And still the tulip lingers,
The wall-flower's red like blood
The ivy spreads pale fingers,
The rose is in the bud.
Good-bye, sweet lilac, and sweet may!
The Rose is on the way.

You were but heralds sent us—
All April's buds, and May's—
But painted missals lent us
That we might learn her praise,

Might cast down every bud that blows
Before our Queen, the Rose!

玫瑰之歌

[英国] 伊迪丝·内斯比特

紫丁香的花期结束，
金链花的时日已过，
红色的山楂花掩映住
太快凋零的白色花朵。
白雪般的绣球悬生之处，
共生着紫色的鸢尾花。

郁金香依然踟蹰未开，
桂竹香嫣红似血
常春藤伸展着苍白的手指，
玫瑰花含苞待放。
再见，甜美的紫丁香和山楂花！
玫瑰即将盛大登场。

你们只是派给我们的信使——
所有四月和五月的蓓蕾——
不过是借给我们的弥撒经书
让我们得以学习对她的赞美，

每朵绽放在她面前的花蕾都低了头，
因为她是我们的王后，玫瑰！

Daffodil
水仙

I Wandered Lonely as a Cloud

By William Wordsworth

I wandered lonely as a cloud
That floats on high o'er vales and hills,
When all at once I saw a crowd,
A host, of golden daffodils;
Beside the lake, beneath the trees,
Fluttering and dancing in the breeze.

Continuous as the stars that shine
And twinkle on the milky way,
They stretched in never-ending line
Along the margin of a bay:
Ten thousand saw I at a glance,
Tossing their heads in sprightly dance.

The waves beside them danced; but they
Out-did the sparkling waves in glee:
A poet could not but be gay,
In such a jocund company:

I gazed—and gazed—but little thought
What wealth the show to me had brought:

For oft, when on my couch I lie
In vacant or in pensive mood,
They flash upon that inward eye
Which is the bliss of solitude;
And then my heart with pleasure fills,
And dances with the daffodils.

我孤独地漫步,像一朵流云

[英国] 威廉·华兹华斯

我孤独地漫步,像一朵流云

高高飘浮在峡谷和群山之上,

忽然之间,我望见大片

群生的金黄水仙;

湖水依偎,树荫庇护,

迎着微风翩然起舞。

如群星璀璨绵延

在银河里闪烁光焰,

它们无边无尽地延展

顺着那湖湾的边缘:

一眼望去,万千朵花,

随风点头,舞姿潇洒。

粼粼波光在花影边荡漾,

但它们的愉悦胜过这波光:

有如此快乐的伙伴在旁,

诗人怎能不心花怒放:

我凝望——凝望——却未料想

这美景予我的财富难以估量：

每当我辗转床榻之上

茫然无计　愁闷神伤，

它们便在我心中闪现

为我的孤苦送来欢畅；

我的心，满溢了喜乐，

同水仙一起　轻舞飞扬。

To an Early Daffodil

by Amy Lowell

Thou yellow trumpeter of laggard Spring!

Thou herald of rich Summer's myriad flowers!

The climbing sun with new recovered powers

Does warm thee into being, through the ring

Of rich, brown earth he woos thee, makes thee fling

Thy green shoots up, inheriting the dowers

Of bending sky and sudden, sweeping showers,

Till ripe and blossoming thou art a thing

To make all nature glad, thou art so gay;

To fill the lonely with a joy untold;

Nodding at every gust of wind to-day,

To-morrow jewelled with raindrops. Always bold

To stand erect, full in the dazzling play

Of April's sun, for thou hast caught his gold.

致早萌的水仙

[美国] 艾米·洛威尔

你是金黄的号手,报送姗姗来迟的春光!
你是繁花的使者,引领绿意葱茏的盛夏!
攀升的太阳用重新恢复的能量
温暖你的生长,他用肥厚的棕色土壤
作为戒指向你求爱,让你的绿色嫩芽
向上萌发,继承了俯身弯曲的天穹,
和倾盆骤降的阵雨作为嫁妆,
直到成熟开花,你才蔚然成景
你如此欢畅,愉悦了所有生灵;
为孤独者注入了无尽的喜悦;
今日随每阵清风点头,
明日戴上雨滴的珠宝。
总是醒目、丰郁,挺立不倒,
迎接四月艳阳的炫目嬉闹,
因为 你已将他的金子纳入怀抱。

Daffodil Time

by Clinton Scollard

It is daffodil time, so the robins all cry,

For the sun's a big daffodil up in the sky,

And when down the midnight the owl calls "to-whoo!"

Why, then the round moon is a daffodil too;

How sheer to the bough-tops the sap starts to climb,

So, merry my masters, it's daffodil time!

It is time for the song; it is time for the sonnet;

It is time for Belinda to have a new bonnet,

All fashioned and furbished with things that are fair,

To rest like a crown on her daffodil hair;

Love beats in the heart like the pulse of a rhyme,

So, merry my masters, it's daffodil time!

It is time when the vales and the hills cry "Away!

Come, join in the joy of the daffodil day!"

For somewhere one waits, with a glow on her face,

With her daffodil smile, and her daffodil grace.

There's a lilt in the air, there's a cheer, there's a chime,
So, merry my masters, it's daffodil time!

水仙时光

[美国]克林顿·斯科拉德

这是水仙时光,知更鸟全部唱响,

因为太阳是大大的黄水仙,盛开在天上,

夜深人静,猫头鹰"突——呜"呼号,

因为圆圆的月儿也是朵黄水仙;

树液陡峭攀升、涌向枝头,

主人们,请纵情欢笑,这是水仙时间!

这是歌唱的时间;是咏诗的时间;

是贝琳达拥有一盏新软帽的时间,

精致的帽子,附带美好的装饰,

像顶王冠,戴在她水仙黄的发丝上;

爱意在心中跃动,像歌韵的脉搏,

主人们,请纵情欢乐,这是水仙时刻!

这时间,溪谷和群山呼唤着"起身!

快来,共享黄水仙日的欢欣!"

唤向某处等待的人儿,她的面孔光彩焕发,

她的仪容似水仙优雅,她的微笑如水仙绽放。

空中传来轻快的曲调、欢呼和钟鸣,
主人们,请纵情欢畅,这是水仙的时光!

In Time of Daffodils

by Edward Estlin Cummings

in time of daffodils (who know
the goal of living is to grow)
forgetting why, remember how

in time of lilacs who proclaim
the aim of waking is to dream,
remember so(forgetting seem)

in time of roses(who amaze
our now and here with paradise)
forgetting if, remember yes

in time of all sweet things beyond
whatever mind may comprehend,
remember seek(forgetting find)

and in a mystery to be
(when time from time shall set us free)
forgetting me,remember me

在水仙花的时节

[美国] 爱德华·埃斯特林·卡明斯

在水仙花的时节（谁会知道
生长才是活着的目标）
忘记为何，记住如何

在丁香花的时节，它们宣称
苏醒的目的是为了入梦，
记住这样（忘记好像）

在玫瑰花的时节，（它们用天堂之美
惊艳了我们的现在）
忘记如果，记住如是

在一切甜美得
超出了理解与想象的时节，
记住寻求（忘记寻得）

在即将来临的神秘里
（当这神秘一次次放我们自由）
把我忘却，把我铭记

注：卡明斯的诗歌原作大都没有大写字母。他常将自己的名字写作"e.e.cummings"。

Daffodil Dawn

by Olive Eleanor Custance

While I slept, and dreamed of you,

Morning, like a princess, came,

All in robe of palest blue:

Stooped and gathered in that hour

From the east a golden flower,

Great and shining flower of flame...

Then she hastened on her way

Singing over plain and hill—

While I slept and dreamed of you

Dreams that never can come true...

Morning at the gates of Day,

Gathered Dawn, the daffodil!

黄水仙黎明

[英国] 奥列佛·艾莉诺·卡斯坦斯

当我睡去,我梦到你,

清晨,像一位公主,驾临,

穿着最素淡的浅蓝色睡裙。

彼时,她轻轻俯身,

从东方采下一枝金色花朵,

硕大而闪耀的火焰花盏……

随即匆匆赶路向前

歌声把山丘与平原传遍——

当我睡去,梦到了你

这美梦永远不会实现……

清晨已来到白昼的门前,

采来了黎明,这株黄水仙!

Where Ships of Purple—Gently Toss

by Emily Dickinson

Where ships of purple—gently toss—

On Seas of Daffodil—

Fantastic Sailors—mingle—

And then—the wharf is still!

紫色的船儿轻轻摇

[美国] 艾米莉·狄金森

黄水仙的花海上——

紫色的船儿——轻轻摇——

美妙的水手走动说笑——

之后——码头静悄悄。

Tulip

郁金香

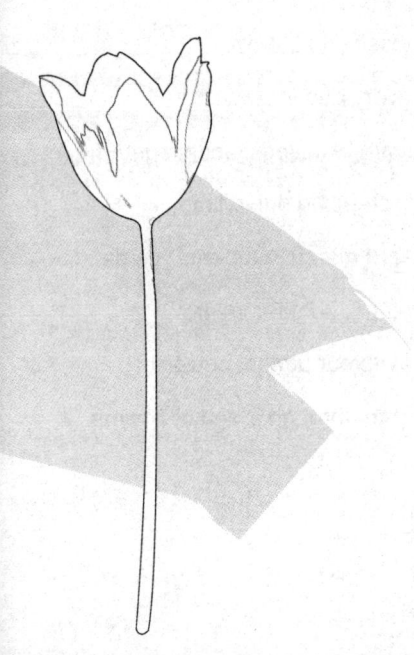

A Tulip Garden

by Amy Lowell

Guarded within the old red wall's embrace,

Marshalled like soldiers in gay company,

The tulips stand arrayed. Here infantry

Wheels out into the sunlight. What bold grace

Sets off their tunics, white with crimson lace!

Here are platoons of gold-frocked cavalry,

With scarlet sabres tossing in the eye

Of purple batteries, every gun in place.

Forward they come, with flaunting colours spread,

With torches burning, stepping out in time

To some quick, unheard march. Our ears are dead,

We cannot catch the tune. In pantomime

Parades that army. With our utmost powers

We hear the wind stream through a bed of flowers.

郁金香花园

[美国]艾米·洛威尔

被老旧的红墙环抱护卫,

像士兵斗志昂扬地集结,

郁金香站立成列。这里

步兵在阳光下展示。多么英勇无畏的风度

衬着他们白底深红花边的　束腰短制服!

这里　是披挂金色外套的骑兵团,

猩红马刀　在紫色排炮的炮眼前晃荡,

每一杆枪　都已准备妥当。

他们向前推进,伸展的色彩招摇,

随行的火炬燃烧,应和着

急速无声的进行曲　踏步而行。

我们的耳朵失灵,无法听到这曲调。

在默剧中检阅这支部队。用尽我们所能

我们只听到了　花坛间穿涌而过的风。

The Tulip Bed

by William Carlos Williams

The May sun—whom

all things imitate—

that glues small leaves to

the wooden trees

shone from the sky

through blue gauze clouds

upon the ground.

Under the leafy trees

where the suburban streets

lay crossed,

with houses on each corner,

tangled shadows had begun

to join

the roadway and the lawns.

With excellent precision

the tulip bed

inside the iron fence

upreared its gaudy

yellow, white and red,
rimmed round with grass,
reposedly.

郁金香花圃

[美国] 威廉·卡洛斯·威廉姆斯

五月的太阳——

万物的效仿对象——

它把些小的叶片

胶粘在木质大树上面。

在天空放射的光芒,

穿过蓝色纱罗的云层

落在大地上。

枝繁叶茂的树下,

郊区的街道

纵横交错,

房屋遍布各个角落,

错综纠缠的阴影

渐渐汇入

路面与草坪。

铁栅栏内,

郁金香花圃

以完美的精心细致,

养育它俗艳花哨的

黄、白、红花朵,

周边绿草环生,

沉静自若。

Hora Stellatrix

by Amy Lowell

The stars hang thick in the apple tree,

The south wind smells of the pungent sea,

Gold tulip cups are heavy with dew.

The night's for you, Sweetheart, for you!

Starfire rains from the vaulted blue.

Listen! The dancing of unseen leaves.

A drowsy swallow stirs in the eaves.

Only a maiden is sorrowing.

'T is night and spring, Sweetheart, and spring!

Starfire lights your heart's blossoming.

In the intimate dark there's never an ear,

Though the tulips stand on tiptoe to hear,

So give; ripe fruit must shrivel or fall.

As you are mine, Sweetheart, give all!

Starfire sparkles, your coronal.

霍拉·史黛拉翠克斯

[美国] 艾米·洛威尔

星星厚重地悬挂在苹果树梢,
南风吹送来浓烈的海洋气息,
郁金香的金色花杯沾满露滴。
这夜晚属于你,亲爱的,属于你!
星火从苍蓝天穹坠落如雨。

听!无人察觉处　树叶飘动。
假寐的燕子在屋檐下微颤。
只有一位少女在忧伤悲叹。
这是春天的夜晚,亲爱的,春天!
星火把你的心花点燃。

隐秘的黑暗里从来没有耳朵,
尽管那郁金香踮起脚尖倾听,
那就给予吧;成熟的果实终将皱缩或掉落。
既然你已属于我,亲爱的,付出一切!
星火在你的冠冕闪烁。

Bulb Planting Time

by Edgar Albert Guest

Last night he said the dead were dead

And scoffed my faith to scorn;

I found him at a tulip bed

When I passed by at morn.

"O ho!" said I, "the frost is near

And mist is on the hills,

And yet I find you planting here

Tulips and daffodils."

"Tis time to plant them now," he said,

"If they shall bloom in Spring";

"But every bulb," said I, "seems dead,

And such an ugly thing."

"The pulse of life I cannot feel,

The skin is dried and brown.

Now look!" a bulb beneath my heel

I crushed and trampled down.

In anger then he said to me:
"You've killed a lovely thing;
A scarlet blossom that would be
Some morning in the Spring."

"Last night a greater sin was thine,"
To him I slowly said;
"You trampled on the dead of mine
And told me they are dead."

球茎种植时间

[美国]埃德加·阿尔伯特·盖思特

昨夜,他说逝者已死,

并嘲弄我的信仰　表达蔑视;

早上我路过郁金香花坛,

发现他就在那里面。

"哦嚯!"我说,"霜冻将至,

雾气在山间盘旋,

我却见你在这种植

郁金香和黄水仙。"

"是时候栽种它们了,"他说,

"如果想让它们开放在春天。"

"但每块球茎,"我说,"都像是死了,

而且如此丑陋不堪。"

"生命的脉搏我感受不到,

外皮干裂,色泽棕暗。

现在　你看!"我用脚跟把球茎踩下,

碾碎并践踏。

他怒气冲冲地对我说：
"你杀死了一个可爱的生灵，
它本可开出猩红的花朵，
在明年春天的某个黎明。"

"昨晚上你的罪过更大，"
我不慌不忙地回敬他，
"你践踏了我的死者，
还对我说　他们已经死了。"

To A Tulip-Bulb

By Edith Nesbit

SLEEP first,

And let the storm and winter do their worst;

Let all the garden lie

Bare to the angry sky,

The shed leaves shiver and die

Above your bed;

Let the white coverlet

Of sunlit snow be set

Over your sleeping head,

While in the earth you sleep

Where dreams are dear and deep,

And heed nor wind nor snow,

Nor how the dark moons go.

In this sad upper world where Winter's hand

Has bound with chains of ice the weary land.

Then wake

To see the whole world lovely for Spring's sake;

The garden fresh and fair

With green things everywhere,

And winter's want and care

Banished and fled;

Primrose and violet

In every border set,

With rain and sunshine fed.

Then bless the fairy song

That cradled you so long,

And bless the fairy kiss

That wakened you to this—

A world where Winter's dead and Spring doth reign

And lovers whisper in the budding lane.

致郁金香球茎

[英国]伊迪丝·内斯比特

首先,沉入睡眠,

让风暴和冬天肆意放纵;

任整个花园平躺,

赤裸地直面愤怒的天空,

蜕落的树叶瑟瑟战栗

在你的花圃上方死去;

让白色的床单

那阳光映照的积雪

笼盖你沉睡的花冠,

此刻,你在泥土中酣睡,

安享甜蜜而深沉的梦境,

不理会那风、那雪,

和黑暗中运行的月。

在这忧伤的上层世界,冬之手

用冰链缚住了疲倦的原野。

然后,苏醒

看全世界明媚可人的春景;

花园清新美丽

处处遍生绿意,

冬天的匮乏忧虑

已被驱逐逃离;

报春花和紫罗兰

在每块花田里生长,

接受雨露阳光滋养。

然后,赞美仙女的歌谣

把你久久拥入怀抱,

赞美仙女的甜吻

把你唤醒,看到这美景——

一个严冬已逝、春光正盛的世界

恋人在花蕾遍布的小路上窃窃私语。

Leaves

by Amelie Rives

Through the leaves of my Tulip tree,

Through the dim, green leaves

Faded by Summer,

Glistens the sky of Autumn;

My thoughts like the leaves are dim,

Faded by memories more passionate

Than the burning of Summer.

Frost will brighten the faded leaves,

But my thoughts will not glow again

Under the frosty touch of age:

Only when Death draws near,

Ardent and luminous,

Will they quicken—

Death that I imagine to be like April sunrise

Through leaves.

叶

[美国] 艾蜜莉·莱夫斯

穿透我郁金香树的花叶,

穿透因炎夏而褪色的

晦暗的绿叶,

照亮秋日的晴空;

我的思绪也如那树叶般晦暗。

是回忆让它们褪色,

这回忆　比夏的灼烧更为狂热。

寒霜会擦亮褪色的叶片,

但岁月的寒霜来袭,

我的思绪不会光辉重现:

只有当死亡降临,

炽热而发亮,

它们才又变得活跃——

这死亡在我想象中　恰似四月的朝阳

穿透树叶。

Violet

紫罗兰

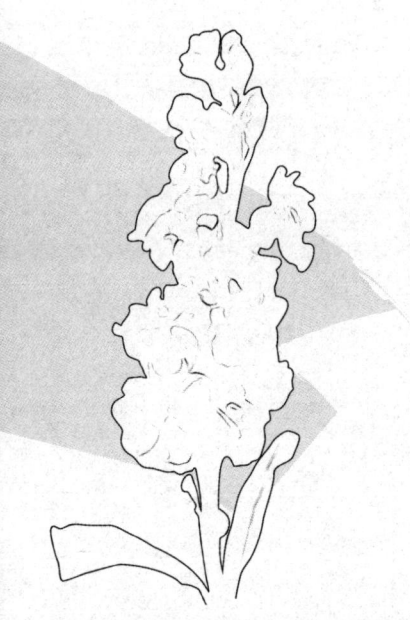

Sweet Violets

by Dorothy Parker

You are brief and frail and blue—

Little sisters, I am, too.

You are Heaven's masterpieces—

Little loves, the likeness ceases.

甜美的紫罗兰

[美国] 多萝西·帕克

你们短命柔弱、忧郁哀伤——
小姐妹们,我也一样。
你们是上天的得意之作——
小可爱们,这点我们不再相仿。

Autumn Violets

By Christina Rossetti

Keep love for youth, and violets for the spring:
Or if these bloom when worn-out autumn grieves,
Let them lie hid in double shade of leaves,
Their own, and others dropped down withering;
For violets suit when home birds build and sing,
Not when the outbound bird a passage cleaves;
Not with dry stubble of mown harvest sheaves,
But when the green world buds to blossoming.
Keep violets for the spring, and love for youth,
Love that should dwell with beauty, mirth, and hope:
Or if a later sadder love be born,
Let this not look for grace beyond its scope,
But give itself, nor plead for answering truth—
A grateful Ruth tho' gleaning scanty corn.

秋日的紫罗兰

[英国] 克里斯蒂娜·罗塞蒂

把爱情留给青春,把紫罗兰留给春光:

若它们在疲惫的秋日陷入悲伤时开放,

那把它们用双层树叶遮蔽隐藏,

它们自己,与其他花一起凋萎沦落;

因为紫罗兰适合在家燕筑巢鸣唱,

绿意盎然的世界含苞待放时生长;

而不是离巢的候鸟远途飞越,

或禾捆收割后留下干谷茬的时节。

把紫罗兰留给春光,把爱情留给青春,

爱情应与美丽、欢笑和希望同驻:

若是有更晚更哀伤的爱情诞生,

别让它在自己视野外寻求恩赐,

也别祈求回复真相,而是给自己一个

拾取稀少谷物的感恩的路得。

注:Ruth(路得),《圣经》中人物,忠心追随一无所有的婆婆娜奥米,在伯利恒靠拾穗生活,后来嫁给了犹太富商波阿斯,是犹太人的国王大卫的祖先。

The Violet

by Jane Taylor

Down in a green and shady bed,
A modest violet grew,
Its stalk was bent, it hung its head,
As if to hide from view.

And yet it was a lovely flower,
Its colours bright and fair;
It might have graced a rosy bower,
Instead of hiding there,

Yet there it was content to bloom,
In modest tints arrayed;
And there diffused a sweet perfume,
Within the silent shade.

Then let me to the valley go,
This pretty flower to see;
That I may also learn to grow
In sweet humility.

紫罗兰

[英国] 珍·泰勒

在一片绿色的阴凉花床,

一株紫罗兰羞答答生长,

花茎弯曲,花冠低垂,

像是为躲避人们的目光。

但它仍美得楚楚可怜,

它的色彩动人明艳;

它本可为玫瑰凉亭增色装点,

而不必默默隐匿此间。

可它却绽放得心满意足,

把自己装扮得淡雅朴素;

寂寂玉立于绿荫之下,

将甜美的芬芳默默飘洒。

让我去往幽静的山谷,

把这俏丽的花儿欣赏;

以让自己也能学会

在恬静淡泊的谦逊中成长。

The Yellow Violet

by William Cullen Bryant

When beechen buds begin to swell,
And woods the blue-bird's warble know,
The yellow violet's modest bell
Peeps from last-year's leaves below.

Ere russet fields their green resume,
Sweet flower, I love, in forest bare,
To meet thee, when thy faint perfume
Alone is in the virgin air.

Of all her train, the hands of Spring
First plant thee in the watery mould,
And I have seen thee blossoming
Beside the snow-bank's edges cold.

Thy parent sun, who bade thee view
Pale skies, and chilling moisture sip
Has bathed thee in his own bright hue,

And streaked with jet thy glowing lip.

Yet slight thy form, and low thy seat,
And earthward bent thy gentle eye,
Unapt the passing view to meet,
When loftier flowers are flaunting nigh.

Oft, in the sunless April day,
Thy early smile has stayed my walk;
But midst the gorgeous blooms of May
I passed thee on thy humble stalk.

So they, who climb to wealth, forget
The friends in darker fortunes tried;
I copied them—but I regret
That I should ape the ways of pride.

And when again the genial hour
Awakes the painted tribes of light,
I'll not o'er look the modest flower
That made the woods of April bright.

黄色紫罗兰

[美国] 威廉·卡伦·布莱恩特

当山毛榉的花蕾开始鼓胀,
蓝鸟在林间鸣啭啾啾,
黄色紫罗兰那羞怯的铃铛
从去年凋落的积叶下探头。

在赤褐色大地返青之前,
于光秃林地,遇见这甜美花朵盛开,
深得我爱,彼时纯净的空气中,
只有你微弱的馨香传来。

春之手,从她的队列
先将你选种于潮湿的土壤,
我还曾见 积雪的河岸边,
你不畏严寒 独自开放。

哺育你的太阳,命令你
仰望苍白的天空,啜饮清冷的湿气;
用他自己的明亮色调为你沐浴,

再用墨玉色条纹，装点你鲜艳的唇。

但你栖身低地，身形瘦纤，
温和的眼神垂向地面，
不惯于迎接路人的眼光，
任高处的花朵炫耀于旁。

在缺少日照的四月天气，
你早绽的笑颜常让我止步伫立；
但在五月绚烂的繁花丛中，
我却踏着你的低矮草茎前行。

有些人坐拥财富、成功向上爬，
就忘记了　朋友还在低迷中挣扎；
我步他们后尘——却又悔恨
自己可笑地模仿了那傲慢之人。

当欢快的时辰　再一次
唤醒光照那鲜艳锦绣的族群，
我不会再轻视这羞怯的小花，
它们照亮了四月的树林。

Wood Violets

by Kate Brownlee Sherwood

Violets, my violets,

Springing from the mould,

From the star-grass and the mosses

Of the woodland dim and old;

Sweet the stories you are telling

Of the fading, happy years,

When the loves were young that vanished

Long ago in mists and tears.

Violets, my violets,

Gazing, I a moment go

Where the moist sweet woody odors

All around me breathe and blow;

Where the bluebells dip their clusters,

And the purple orchids hide;

And, with heart grown strangely happy,

Fling my burdens all aside.

Violets, my violets,

There was once a child that flew

Through the depths of field and forest,

Searching patiently for you;

And that child who now so wearies

Of the fairest thing that grows,

Once grew wild with rapture finding

But a single woodland rose.

Violets, my violets,

If you knew how dark and chill

All our fair young world is growing,

Could you bloom so lovely still?

Could you waken hopes that, flying,

Swiftly fall with broken wings,

If you knew a time of dying

Stills the sweetest voice that sings?

Violets, my violets,

It is but a little boon:

Bend your kindly eyes above me,

When I go, or late, or soon;

And perchance some sad one going

Through the forests of the dead,

Shall remember where I'm sleeping,

By the violets at my head.

林地紫罗兰

[美国] 凯特·布朗利·舍伍德

紫罗兰,我的紫罗兰,
萌生于土壤里,
幽暗古老的林地
那片星星草和苔藓里;
你诉说着甜蜜的往事
逐渐褪色的欢乐岁月,
年轻的爱情,很久之前
消失在迷雾和泪水之间。

紫罗兰,我的紫罗兰,
片刻之前,我静心凝视
那里,湿润甜美的木香
在我身旁呼吸吹动;
那里,蓝铃花垂着花簇,
紫色兰藏身草丛;
我的心变得莫名喜悦,
将所有烦扰全部抛却。

紫罗兰,我的紫罗兰,

曾经有一个孩童

飞越田野和森林深处,

耐心把你找寻;

他曾经变得欣喜若狂,

只因孤零零一朵林地蔷薇,

现在　却对最美丽的生灵

都深感寡淡无味。

紫罗兰,我的紫罗兰,

若你知道　这世界的美丽朝气

已渐渐被黑暗与凄寒代替,

你是否还能　静静地吐露芳华?

若你知道命数将尽、死亡来临

甜美的歌喉不能再欢唱,

你是否还能　唤醒飞行途中

那迅速跌落而折翼的希望?

紫罗兰,我的紫罗兰,

我只求一个小小的恩惠:

将你友善的眼睛向我低垂,

当我离开,或迟、或快;

也许会有伤心之人

穿过这逝者的森林,

还能记得我长眠的地方,

头顶有紫罗兰开放。

Iris

鸢尾

Flame. Yellow-Iris

by Frances Sargent Osgood

YELLOW-IRIS.

The German peasant wreathes his roof with flower in rich attire,
For sun-tressed Iris waves for him her urns of fragrant fire:
But we have let a holier gem our lowly home illume—
The flower of love our lattice lights with undecaying bloom.

火焰.黄色鸢尾花

[美国]弗朗西斯·萨金特·奥斯古德

黄色鸢尾。
德国村夫盛装打扮,为他的屋顶装饰鲜花花环,
用阳光梳妆的鸢尾,朝他挥舞芬芳如火的花冠:
但我们有更圣洁的宝贝,让我们家蓬荜生辉——
爱的花朵不朽绽放,把我们的花格窗点亮。

Sea Iris

by Hilda Doolittle

I

Weed, moss-weed,

root tangled in sand,

sea-iris, brittle flower,

one petal like a shell

is broken,

and you print a shadow

like a thin twig.

Fortunate one,

scented and stinging,

rigid myrrh-bud,

camphor-flower,

sweet and salt—you are wind

in our nostrils.

II

Do the murex-fishers

drench you as they pass?

Do your roots drag up colour

from the sand?

Have they slipped gold under you—

rivets of gold?

Band of iris-flowers

above the waves,

you are painted blue,

painted like a fresh prow

stained among the salt weeds.

海鸢尾

[美国] 希尔达·杜利特尔

一

水草,苔样水草,

根须缠结在沙里,

海鸢尾,脆弱的花朵,

花瓣一枚,似贝壳

破碎,

你烙印的影子,

仿若纤瘦的细枝。

幸运儿啊,

浓香散溢、强烈刺人,

花苞清冷如没药,

花朵气味似樟脑,

甜咸交融——你是风

钻进我们的鼻孔。

二

骨骡渔民经过时

会不会把你淋湿?
你的根须会不会
从沙滩里拖拽出颜色?
他们会不会在你身下偷放金子——
金子的铆钉?

成片的鸢尾花
漂浮于海浪之上,
你们被涂成湛蓝,
像崭新的船首
在腥咸的水草中,污迹斑斑。

Poppy Seed—In a Garden

by Amy Lowell

Gushing from the mouths of stone men

To spread at ease under the sky

In granite-lipped basins,

Where iris dabble their feet

And rustle to a passing wind,

The water fills the garden with its rushing,

In the midst of the quiet of close-clipped lawns.

Damp smell the ferns in tunnels of stone,

Where trickle and plash the fountains,

Marble fountains, yellowed with much water.

Splashing down moss-tarnished steps

It falls, the water;

And the air is throbbing with it.

With its gurgling and running.

With its leaping, and deep, cool murmur.

And I wished for night and you.

I wanted to see you in the swimming-pool,

White and shining in the silver-flecked water.

While the moon rode over the garden,

High in the arch of night,

And the scent of the lilacs was heavy with stillness.

Night, and the water, and you in your whiteness, bathing!

罂粟种子——在花园里

[美国] 艾米·洛威尔

从石像的口中喷涌而出,
在天空下悠然铺展。
花岗岩的唇形盆中,
鸢尾花用脚丫戏水,
随风吹沙沙作响,
水用急流充满了整个花园,
在修剪整齐的草坪的寂静里。

蕨类在石缝中散发潮湿气息,
喷泉在那儿涓流泼溅,
大理石喷泉,因大量流水而泛黄。

水流迸溅,
淌落下青苔滋生的阶梯;
空气也随之悸动。
伴随着它的汩汩奔涌。
伴随着它的跳跃,和低沉清凉的低吟。

我希望得到黑夜和你。
我想在游泳池中见到你,
在银光点点的水上,洁白而闪亮。
当月亮掠过花园,
高悬于黑夜的拱门,
紫丁香的香气因静滞而浓郁。

黑夜,水,和洁白之中沐浴的你!

The France Flower

by John Galsworthy

I stroll forth this flowery day

Of "print frocks" and buds of may,

And speedwells of tender blue

Whom no sky can match for hue.

I love well my English home;

Yet far thoughts do stealing come

To throng me like honey-bees,

Till far flowers my fancy sees—

'Tis almond against the snows,

And gentian, and mountain rose,

And iris, in purple bright,

The France flower, the flower of light!

法国之花

[英国] 约翰·高尔斯华绥

我在这繁花盛开的时节

漫步于"印花衣裳"和五月的蓓蕾,

婆婆纳的嫩蓝花色

天空的色调也无法媲美。

我深爱我的英国家园;

但遥远的思念偷偷袭来,

如蜜蜂一般簇拥着我,

直到我用幻想看到远方的花朵——

那是杏花映照着白雪,

龙胆花和山玫瑰,

还有鲜艳的紫色鸢尾,

法国之花,光之花卉!

Iris

by Louise Driscoll

Now iris, like a flock of birds,
Down to the pool's green water flies,
Sunning small, lovely, curving wings
And radiant, scented dyes.
As in a mirror, on the pool
The gold and purple lies.

I waited, hoping for a song,
I saw the tall leaves bend and swing,
It seemed to me some violet throat
Might open presently and sing,
But they were still as birds at night,
Each with his head beneath his wing.

鸢尾花

[美国] 露易丝·德里斯科尔

眼下,鸟群般的鸢尾,

飞掠一池碧水,

晾着纤巧弯曲的羽翼,

明亮的色调带着香气。

金黄和湛紫的花躺卧池上,

就像是在镜里。

我等待,盼望有歌声传来,

我看到高处的叶子弯折摇摆,

仿若紫罗兰的喉咙

马上要张开,唱响,

但它们安静得像夜间的鸟,

将脑袋在翅膀下深藏。

On Such a Day

by Mary Elizabeth Coleridge

Some hang above the tombs,

Some weep in empty rooms,

I, when the iris blooms,

Remember.

I, when the cyclamen

Opens her buds again,

Rejoice a moment—then

Remember.

在这样的日子里

[英国] 玛丽·伊丽莎白·柯勒律治

有人悬挂于坟墓上方,
有人在空荡的房间哭泣,
而我,当鸢尾花盛放,
便陷入回忆。

当仙客来
再度把她的花蕾绽开,
我,欣喜片刻后——
便开始追怀。

Not Iris in Her Pride

by George Peele

Not Iris in her pride and bravery
Adorns her arch with such variety;
Nor doth the Milk-white Way in frosty night
Appear so fair and beautiful in sight,
As do these fields and groves and sweetest bowers
Bestrewed and decked with parti-coloured flowers.
Along the bubbling brooks and silver glide,
That at the bottom doth in silence slide,
The water-flowers and lilies on the banks
Like blazing comets burgeon all in ranks;
Under the hawthorn and the poplar tree,
Where sacred Phoebe may delight to be,
The primrose and the purple hyacinth,
The dainty violet and the wholesome minth,
The double-daisy and the cowslip (Queen)
Of summer flowers) do over-peer the green;
And round about the valley as ye pass,
Ye may not see, for peeping flowers, the grass.

矜傲的鸢尾花不会……

[英国]乔治·皮尔

矜傲无畏的鸢尾花不会

为她的拱瓣作如此繁复的点缀；

霜夜的乳白色路面

也不会看上去如此美丽优雅；

不像这田野、树林和无比宜人的树荫

用五色斑驳的花朵，将自己装扮铺满。

沿着冒泡的溪涧，和银亮亮的

于水底清寂处滑行的静流，

水生花卉和岸边的百合

如绚烂的彗星，成群速生。

在山楂树和白杨树下，

神圣的菲比或许会心悦此地，

报春花、紫色风信子、

雅致的紫罗兰、有益的薄荷草、

双瓣雏菊和莲馨花（夏花的女王）

摇曳于绿草上面；

在整个峡谷开遍，当你漫步其中，

可能不见草叶，因繁花隐约显现。

注：Phoebe（菲比），希腊神话中的月亮女神，是天空之神乌拉诺斯和大地之神盖亚的女儿。

Scent of Irises

by David Herbert Lawrence

A faint, sickening scent of irises

Persists all morning. Here in a jar on the table

A fine proud spike of purple irises

Rising above the class-room litter, makes me unable

To see the class's lifted and bended faces

Save in a broken pattern, amid purple and gold and sable.

I can smell the gorgeous bog-end, in its breathless

Dazzle of may-blobs, when the marigold glare overcast you

With fire on your cheeks and your brow and your chin as you dipped

Your face in the marigold bunch, to touch and contrast you,

Your own dark mouth with the bridal faint lady-smocks,

Dissolved on the golden sorcery you should not outlast.

You amid the bog-end's yellow incantation,
You sitting in the cowslips of the meadow above,
Me, your shadow on the bog-flame, flowery may-blobs,
Me full length in the cowslips, muttering you love;
You, your soul like a lady-smock, lost, evanescent,
You with your face all rich, like the sheen of a dove.

You are always asking, do I remember, remember
The butter-cup bog-end where the flowers rose up
And kindled you over deep with a cast of gold?
You ask again, do the healing days close up
The open darkness which then drew us in,
The dark which then drank up our brimming cup.

You upon the dry, dead beech-leaves, in the fire of night

Burnt like a sacrifice; you invisible;

Only the fire of darkness, and the scent of you!

—And yes, thank God, it still is possible

The healing days shall close the darkness up

Wherein we fainted like a smoke or dew.

Like vapour, dew, or poison. Now, thank God,

The fire of night is gone, and your face is ash

Indistinguishable on the grey, chill day;

The night had burst us out, at last the good

Dark fire burns on untroubled, without clash

Of you upon the dead leaves saying me Yea.

鸢尾花香

[英国] 戴维·赫伯特·劳伦斯

一股淡淡的令人作呕的鸢尾花香
持续了整个早上。桌上这只罐子里
纤巧而高傲的紫色鸢尾花穗
升起于教室的凌乱上方,让我无法
看清班里那些抬起或垂下的面容
只有破碎的图案,混杂于紫、金、黑色之中。

我能闻到华丽的沼泽尽端,马蹄草炫目耀眼
让人惊叹,当你把脸埋入万寿菊的花束,
它用眩光笼罩了你,让你的脸颊、眉毛和下巴
燃起火焰,那新娘般素淡的碎米荠
与你的深色嘴唇对比碰触,
便消散于流传久远的金色巫术。

你在沼泽尽头的黄色咒语之间,
你在上方草甸的莲馨花丛之中,
我,你落在沼泽火焰,那绚烂马蹄草上的影子,
我伸直躺倒在莲馨花里,向你低语爱意;
你,你的灵魂像朵碎米荠,瞬息消散、失落迷离,

你的面容美丽动人，亮泽如一只白鸽。

你总是问我，是否记得，记得
毛茛花茂密生长在沼泽尽头
用一捧金色把你彻底点燃？
你又问，疗愈的岁月是否关上
将我们深深吸引的　敞开的黑暗，
这黑暗，彼时饮干了我们满溢的杯盏。

你在枯死的山毛榉叶上，在暗夜之火里
献祭般燃烧；又消失不见；
只余黑暗的火焰，和你的香氛！
——是啊，感谢上帝，这可能依然尚存
疗愈的岁月将关闭黑暗之门，
如烟似露，我们在那里昏倒。

如蒸汽、露水或毒药。现在，感谢上帝，
黑夜之火已熄，而你的脸化为灰烬
在灰暗阴冷的白昼里难以辨认；
黑夜把我们烧尽，最终
迷人的暗火继续烧，无人打扰，
没有你撞击着枯叶对我说"是的"。

Lilac

紫丁香

When Lilacs Last in the Dooryard Bloomed

by Walt Whitman

When lilacs last in the dooryard bloomed
And the great star early drooped in the western sky in the night,
I mourned, and yet shall mourn with ever-returning spring.

Ever-returning spring, trinity sure to me you bring,
Lilac blooming perennial and drooping star in the west,
And thought of him I love.

当紫丁香最后一次在庭院开放

[美国] 沃尔特·惠特曼

当紫丁香最后一次在庭院开放
那颗伟大的星辰提早坠落于西方的夜空,
我哀痛,并将在年年复归的春天永远哀痛。

年年复归的春天,你必为我带来这三位一体:
岁岁花开的紫丁香,西方坠落的星辰,
和我对那敬爱之人的追思怀念。

The Lilac

by Humbert Wolfe

Who thought of the lilac?

"I," dew said,

"I made up the lilac,

out of my head."

"She made up the lilac!

Pooh!" thrilled a linnet,

and each dew-note had a lilac in it

紫丁香

[英国] 亨伯特·沃尔夫

是谁想出了紫丁香?
"是我,"露珠说,
"我从我的脑海中,
创造出了紫丁香。"

"她创造了紫丁香!
呸!"朱顶雀激动叫嚷。
每滴露珠音符,都显映出一朵丁香。

A Song of the Lilac

by Louise Imogen Guiney

Above the wall that's broken,

And from the coppice thinned,

So sacred and so sweet

The lilac in the wind!

And when by night the May wind blows

The lilac-blooms apart,

The memory of his first love

Is shaken on his heart.

In tears it long was buried,

And trances wrapt it round;

O how they wake it now,

The fragrance and the sound!

For when by night the May wind blows

The lilac-blooms apart,

The memory of his first love

Is shaken on his heart.

紫丁香之歌

[美国] 露易丝·伊莫金·吉尼

于残垣断壁上方,

从稀疏的矮树丛中生长,

那么圣洁端庄、甜美芬芳,

风中摇曳的紫丁香!

当五月的晚风

把丁香花簇吹散,

对初恋的回忆

让他心神难安。

这回忆早已被泪水埋葬,

恍惚出神将它缠裹隐藏;

哦,它现在却被唤醒,

只因这香气和声响!

当五月的晚风

把丁香花簇吹散,

对初恋的回忆

让他心神难安。

Somebody Brought in Lilac

by Lesbia Harford

Somebody brought in lilac,

Lilac after rain.

Isn't it strange, beloved of mine

You'll not see it again?

Lilac glad with the sun on it

Flagrant fair from birth,

Mourns in colour, beloved of mine,

You laid in the earth.

有人送来了丁香花

[澳大利亚] 莱斯比亚·哈福德

有人送来了丁香花,

一支雨后的丁香花。

多么奇怪,心爱的人,

你再也不能看到它。

紫丁香愉快地迎接太阳,

她天生丽质　馥郁芬芳。

用颜色把哀思倾诉,心爱的人,

如今你已躺卧泥土。

Orchid
兰花

At Baia

by Hilda Doolittle

I should have thought

in a dream you would have brought

some lovely, perilous thing,

orchids piled in a great sheath,

as who would say (in a dream),

"I send you this,

who left the blue veins

of your throat unkissed."

Why was it that your hands

(that never took mine),

your hands that I could see

drift over the orchid-heads

so carefully,

your hands, so fragile, sure to lift

so gently, the fragile flower-stuff—

ah, ah, how was it

You never sent (in a dream)

the very form, the very scent,

not heavy, not sensuous,

but perilous—perilous—

of orchids, piled in a great sheath,

and folded underneath on a bright scroll,

some word:

"Flower sent to flower;

for white hands, the lesser white,

less lovely of flower-leaf,"

or

"Lover to lover, no kiss,

no touch, but forever and ever this."

在巴亚

[美国] 希尔达·杜利特尔

我应该想到

梦里,你会带来

一些可爱而危险的东西,

兰花簇拥在巨大的叶鞘里,

正如有人会说(在梦里):

"我把这送给你,

它不会在你喉咙的青筋

烙上唇印。"

为什么,你的双手

(从不曾牵过我),

我能看到的这双手

小心翼翼地

拂过兰花的蕊头,

你的手,如此纤巧,抬起得

如此轻柔,这娇弱的花朵——

啊,啊,这是为何

你从未送来（在梦里）

这样的形态，这样的香气，

不浓烈沉郁，不摄人心神，

而是危险的——危险的——

兰花，簇拥在巨大的叶鞘里，

一些文字，

折叠于鲜艳的卷轴之上：

"把花朵赠予花朵；

白皙素手，把花叶衬得

雪白黯淡　姿容减色。"

或是

"将情人送予情人，无法亲吻，

不能触摸，如此相伴，直到永远。"

Orchids

by Theodore Wratislaw

Orange and purple, shot with white and mauve,
Such in a greenhouse wet with tropic heat
One sees these delicate flowers whose parents throve
In some Pacific island's hot retreat.

Their ardent colours that betray the rank
Fierce hotbed of corruption whence they rose
Please eyes that long for stranger sweets than prank
Wild meadow-blooms and what the garden shows.

Exotic flowers! How great is my delight
To watch your petals curiously wrought,
To lie among your splendours day and night
Lost in a subtle dream of subtler thought.

Bathed in your clamorous orchestra of hues,

The palette of your perfumes, let me sleep

While your mesmeric presences diffuse

Weird dreams: and then bizarre sweet rhymes shall creep

Forth from my brain and slowly form and make

Sweet poems as a weaving spider spins,

A shrine of loves that laugh and swoon and ache,

A temple of coloured sorrows and perfumed sins!

兰花

[英国] 西奥多·拉蒂斯劳

橙色、紫色,夹杂白和淡紫,
人们在因热带高温而潮湿的暖房
见到这娇嫩的花朵,它们的祖先曾繁茂生长
在某个太平洋岛屿的避暑幽静之乡。

热烈的色彩,暴露了它们滋生的
恶臭难闻且腐败糟糕的温床,
取悦了那些渴望陌生人的糖果,而非
调笑的草地野花和花园美景的眼光。

异域风情的花草! 我多么欢喜
当我看到　你花瓣那奇异的锻造,
日夜躺卧于你的光彩,迷失在
微妙梦境,这梦境有关更微妙的思考。

浸泡于你纷乱管弦般的色调,
你的香气调色板,催我入眠
你令人着迷的存在弥散出

奇怪的梦：然后诡异甜美的韵律渐渐

在我的脑海里浮现，把优美的诗
慢慢创作构思，仿若蜘蛛纺线吐丝，
欢笑、昏倒、疼痛，一方爱的圣坛，
一座悲伤焕彩、罪恶飘香的神殿！

Jasmine
茉莉花

Jasmines

by Claude McKay

Your scent is in the room.

Swiftly it overwhelms and conquers me!

Jasmines, night jasmines, perfect of perfume,

Heavy with dew before the dawn of day!

Your face was in the mirror. I could see

You smile and vanish suddenly away,

Leaving behind the vestige of a tear.

Sad suffering face, from parting grown so dear!

Night jasmines cannot bloom in this cold place;

Without the street is wet and weird with snow;

The cold nude trees are tossing to and fro;

Too stormy is the night for your fond face;

For your low voice too loud the wind's mad roar.

But oh, your scent is here—jasmines that grow

Luxuriant, clustered round your cottage door!

茉莉花

[美国] 克劳德·麦凯

你的香气在房间里。

它迅速淹没并征服了我!

茉莉,夜茉莉,花香绝美,

在拂晓前沾满湿重的露水!

镜中是你的面容。我能看到

你微微一笑　又倏然形消,

只余存一抹泪痕。

愁苦的面容,离别后愈显珍重!

夜茉莉无法绽放在这苦寒之地;

没有它,积雪的街道潮湿诡异;

受冻的裸露树木来回晃动;

于你温情的面容,夜的风暴太肆虐;

于你低柔的声音,风的狂啸太剧烈。

可是,哦,这里有你的香气——茉莉,

郁郁葱葱,在你的小屋门旁丛生!

注:night jasmine(夜茉莉),即夜香木,也叫夜来香,一种常绿灌木,花芳香,夜间尤盛。

The First Jasmines

by Rabindranath Tagore

Ah, these jasmines, these white jasmines!

I seem to remember the first day when I filled my hands with these jasmines, these white jasmines.

I have loved the sunlight, the sky and the green earth;

I have heard the liquid murmur of the river thorough the darkness of midnight;

Autumn sunsets have come to me at the bend of a road in the lonely waste, like a bride raising her veil to accept her lover.

Yet my memory is still sweet with the first white jasmines

that I held in my hands when I was a child.

Many a glad day has come in my life, and I have laughed with merrymakers on festival nights.

On grey mornings of rain I have crooned many an idle song.

I have worn round my neck the evening wreath of

bakulas woven by the hand of love.

Yet my heart is sweet with the memory of the first fresh jasmines that filled my hands when I was a child.

第一次的茉莉

[印度] 罗宾德拉纳特·泰戈尔

啊,这些茉莉,这些纯白的茉莉!

我仿佛想起双手捧起这茉莉的第一天,

这纯白的茉莉。

我深爱阳光、天空和苍翠的大地;

我倾听河流,在幽暗的午夜柔声低语;

秋日的夕阳,在孤寂荒野的

小路弯折处迎我,像一位新娘,

撩起面纱,迎接情郎。

可是,儿时的记忆依旧甜蜜,

那些我第一次双手捧起的白色茉莉。

我平生度过了许多愉快时光,

节庆之夜,与纵情欢乐者笑声朗朗。

落雨的晦暗清晨,把悠闲的小曲浅吟低唱。

爱人亲手用醉花编织的黄昏花环,

佩戴于我脖颈之上。

可是,儿时的记忆依旧甜蜜,

那些我第一次双手捧起的清新茉莉。

Lily
百合

The Lily

by William Blake

The modest Rose puts forth a thorn,

The humble sheep a threat'ning horn:

While the Lily white shall in love delight,

Nor a thorn nor a threat stain her beauty bright.

百合花

[英国] 威廉·布莱克

羞怯的蔷薇长出尖锐的刺,
温驯的羔羊顶着威胁的角:
而洁白的百合沉浸于爱的欢喜,
没有尖刺和长角来玷污她的明丽。

The Lily and the Bee

by Henry Lawson

I Looked upon the lilies
When the morning sun was low,
And the sun shone through a lily
With a softened honey glow.
A spot was in the lily
That moved incessantly,
And when I looked into the cup
I saw a morning bee.
"Consider the lilies!"
But, it occurs to me,
Does any one consider
The lily and the bee?

The lily stands for beauty,
Use, purity, and trust,
It does a four-fold duty,
As all good mortals must.
Its whiteness is to teach us,

Its faith to set us free,

Its beauty is to cheer us,

And its wealth is for the bee.

"Consider the lilies!"

But, it occurs to me,

Does any one consider

The lily and the bee?

百合与蜜蜂

[澳大利亚] 亨利·劳森

我望着百合花丛

当清晨的太阳尚低,

晨曦透过一支百合

散发柔和的蜜色光泽。

百合中有个斑点

在不停歇地挪动,

我看向花杯的内侧

发现是只晨间的蜜蜂。

"百合值得细想!"

但我突然意识到,

这百合与蜜蜂

有没有人关注?

百合代表美丽、

用途、纯洁和信任,

它承担了这四重天职,

所有良善的凡人都必须如此。

它的洁白为教导我们,

它的信仰为给我们自由,

它的美丽为愉悦我们,

它的财富为造福蜜蜂。

"百合值得细想!"

但我突然意识到

这百合与蜜蜂

有没有人关注?

A Lyric to Lily

by Charles Henry Webb

If I were a honey-bee

What would I do?

I'll tell to no other,

Darling, but you:

Near the heart of the Lily,

Folding my wings,—

Think it no harm, darling,

'T is a bee sings,—

There I would linger

All of the day;

None of the garden

Should tempt me away.

The Tulip, proud lady,

I would disdain;

The Violet's blue eyes should

Woo me in vain;

The tears of the Blue-bell

Ever might fall;

The Rose and the Woodbine

Cling to the wall;

The Cowslip and Daisy

Lie in the sun:

I would not kiss them,—

Never a one.

But alone with my Lily

Ever I'd rest,

Shrined in the whiteness

Of her fair breast;

Think it no harm, darling,—

Only you see

That I'd make honey

Were I a bee!

献给百合的抒情诗

[美国] 查尔斯·亨利·韦伯

如果我是只蜜蜂

我会做什么?

我不会告诉别人,

亲爱的,除了你:

靠近百合的心脏、

收起我的翅膀——

这没有妨害,亲爱的,

只是蜜蜂在歌唱——

我愿在那儿逗留

整日流连徘徊;

花园里的一切

都无法诱我离开。

郁金香那傲慢小姐,

我只会轻视鄙弃;

紫罗兰的湛蓝媚眼

也徒劳求我怜爱;

蓝铃花的泪珠
随时可能滴落；
蔷薇与五叶地锦
紧紧贴附墙壁；
莲馨花与雏菊
躺卧在阳光里：
我不会亲吻它们——
一个吻也不给。

我要和我的百合一起
独自守着她栖息，
依偎她白皙美丽的胸脯
像是身居圣地；
这并无妨害，亲爱的，
只是你懂，
我会酿造花蜜，
若我是只蜜蜂！

Loneliness

by Danske Bedinger Dandridge

A lily alone in a border of Roses:
I saw her lean forward her beautiful head;
And the breezes were rich with the breath of her longing,
Sweet grief wafted o'er to the Lily-bed.

There grew the bright Lilies, the fresh, golden Lilies;
They caught the warm light in each exquisite flower:
Did they catch the faint fragrance the breeze wafted over?
Did they dream of their mate in the Roses' bower?

Alas! the meek stranger, alone 'mid her rivals!
I waited the end with a pitying sigh:
I saw her droop forward, away from the Roses,
And lean toward the Lilies, and wither, and die.

But when the last petal had faded and fallen
Among the soft Rose-leaves, blush, amber, and red,
Did the free Lily-spirit escape to her sisters?
Did the breeze waft her o'er to the Lily-bed?

孤独

[美国] 丹斯克·贝丁格·丹德里奇

一支百合独生于玫瑰花丛:
我见她将美丽的花冠前倾;
微风中弥漫着她渴望的气息,
甜蜜的忧伤飘向百合的花床。

那里生着亮丽的百合,明净的金色百合;
那精致的花朵,在和煦的光线中闪烁:
它们是否闻到了微风吹送来的幽香?
它们是否梦到了玫瑰花荫中的伙伴?

唉!这怯弱的陌生者,在对手中茕茕孑立,
我带着遗憾的叹息,等待她的结局:
我见她背对着玫瑰低垂,
朝向百合倾斜,随后凋萎。

但当最后一片花瓣褪色,坠落于
泛着红晕、琥珀色和红色的柔软花叶,
自由的百合灵魂是否逃到了姐妹身边?
微风是否把她吹送到百合的花田?

Waterlily

莲花

Water Lilies

by Sara Teasdale

If you have forgotten water lilies floating
On a dark lake among mountains in the afternoon shade,
If you have forgotten their wet, sleepy fragrance,
Then you can return and not be afraid.

But if you remember, then turn away forever
To the plains and the prairies where pools are far apart,
There you will not come at dusk on closing water lilies,
And the shadow of mountains will not fall on your heart.

睡莲

[美国] 萨拉·提斯黛尔

若你已忘记睡莲漂浮于幽暗的湖面
在笼罩于午后暗影的群山之间,
若你已忘记她们潮湿且欲眠的芬芳,
那么,你可以回来,无须畏惧心慌。

但若是你还记得,那就永远离开,
去往平地与草原那远离池塘的地带,
那里你不会遇见随暮色闭合的睡莲,
山峦的阴影也不会投映在你的心涧。

Water Lily

by Rainer Maria Rilke

My whole life is mine, but whoever says so
will deprive me, for it is infinite.
The ripple of water, the shade of the sky
are mine; it is still the same, my life.

No desire opens me: I am full,
I never close myself with refusal—
in the rythm of my daily soul
I do not desire—I am moved;

by being moved I exert my empire,
making the dreams of night real:
into my body at the bottom of the water
I attract the beyonds of mirrors...

睡莲

[奥地利] 莱纳·玛利亚·里尔克

我的整个生命都属于我,可谁若这么说

就是对我的剥夺,因为它无穷无限。

水的涟漪,天空的投影,都属于我;

而我的生命如常,不增不减。

欲望不能让我开放:我本就圆满,

我从不用拒绝来封闭自己——

在我日常灵魂的律动中

我没有欲求——我只受感动;

经由感动,我行使自己的君权,

把夜晚的梦想实现:

在我的身体里,于那幽深水底,

我吸引着 镜子以外的边际……

The Lotus

by Rabindranath Tagore

On the day when the lotus bloomed, alas, my mind was straying,
and I knew it not. My basket was empty and the flower remained unheeded.

Only now and again a sadness fell upon me, and I started up from my dream and felt a sweet trace of a strange fragrance in the south wind.

That vague sweetness made my heart ache with longing and it seemed to me that is was the eager breath of the summer seeking for its completion.

I knew not then that it was so near, that it was mine, and that this perfect sweetness had blossomed in the depth of my own heart.

莲花

[印度] 罗宾德拉纳特·泰戈尔

莲花开放的那天,唉,我的心神游离飞飘,
自己却不知晓。我花篮空空,对那花朵却未留意。

然而一缕哀愁　时而落上心头,我从睡梦中惊起,
闻到南风里　一丝甜美而奇异的香气。

这朦胧的芳香　让我因想望而心痛,在我看来
这似乎是夏日　寻求完满的热切气息。

那时我还不知道,它近在身旁,并属于我,
这完美的甜香,已在我内心深处开放。

Daisy

雏菊

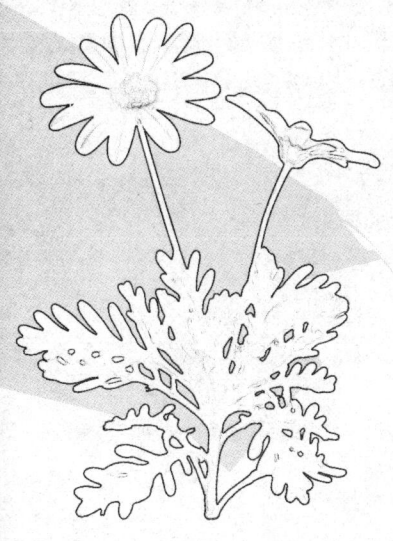

So Has A Daisy Vanished

by Emily Dickinson

So has a Daisy vanished

From the fields today—

So tiptoed many a slipper

To Paradise away—

Oozed so in crimson bubbles

Day's departing tide—

Blooming—tripping—flowing

Are ye then with God?

一朵雏菊就这样消失

[美国]艾米莉·狄金森

一朵雏菊今天就这样

消失于原野上——

许多便鞋轻手蹑脚

奔赴天堂——

渗冒着深红色泡沫

那白昼离去的潮汐——

绽放——轻跃——流淌——

你是否见到了上帝?

The Daisy Follows Soft the Sun

by Emily Dickinson

The Daisy follows soft the Sun—

And when his golden walk is done—

Sits shyly at his feet—

He—waking—finds the flower there—

Wherefore—Marauder—art thou here?

Because, Sir, love is sweet!

We are the Flower—Thou the Sun!

Forgive us, if as days decline—

We nearer steal to Thee!

Enamored of the parting West—

The peace—the flight—the Amethyst—

Night's possibility!

雏菊轻柔地追随太阳

[美国] 艾米莉·狄金森

雏菊轻柔地追随太阳——

当他的金色漫步结束——

便羞怯地坐在他脚旁——

他——醒来——发现了那里的雏菊

这是为何——劫掠者——你在这里?

因为,先生,爱意如此甜蜜!

我们是花朵——你是太阳!

原谅我们,若随着日色消减——

我们悄悄地接近你!

迷恋那作别的西方天际——

平静——飞逝——紫水晶——

夜的可能情形!

Daisy Time

by Marjorie Pickthall

See, the grass is full of stars,
Fallen in their brightness;
Hearts they have of shining gold,
Rays of shining whiteness.

Buttercups have honeyed hearts,
Bees they love the clover,
But I love the daisies' dance
All the meadow over.

Blow, O blow, you happy winds,
Singing summer's praises,
Up the field and down the field
A-dancing with the daisies.

雏菊时节

[加拿大]玛乔丽·皮克索尔

看,草丛里满是繁星,

于光明中坠落;

它们的心闪耀如金,

白亮的光芒闪烁。

毛茛有蜜色的花心,

蜜蜂钟爱三叶草,

而我喜欢雏菊花

在整片草地上的舞蹈。

吹吧,哦吹吧,欢乐的风,

把夏日的赞歌吟咏,

在田野上来来回回

同雏菊翩翩舞动。

Little Daisy

by Jurgis Baltrušaitis

Little daisy, white as snow,
To delight me as I tread,
From the roadside dust you grow,
Lifting up your pretty head.

Under sorrow's weight I groaned;
Your sweet flower healed my sore.
In the world I'm not alone,
Not an orphan any more.

Poverty seems to be gone,
Gone the pain, and life seems worth
Living – not like exile on
This dark, melancholy earth.

With sunshine you filled my heart,
And I walk along, made bold
By the song bereft of art
You left singing in my soul.

小雏菊

[立陶宛] 尤吉斯·巴楚萨蒂斯

小雏菊,洁白似雪,
走在上面让我心欢,
你生于路边的尘土,
高昂着美丽的花冠。

我在悲伤的重压下呻吟;
你甜美的花朵疗愈我的伤心。
在这个世界上,我不再孤独,
不再像个孤儿,独自凄苦。

贫穷似乎已经消失,
一如痛苦,生命似乎值得
活着——而不再是像
在这黑暗忧郁的大地上流放。

你让我的心灵充满阳光,
我勇敢无畏地走向前方,
因你把那去除艺术雕琢的歌曲
在我的灵魂深处唱响。

Rosemary

迷迭香

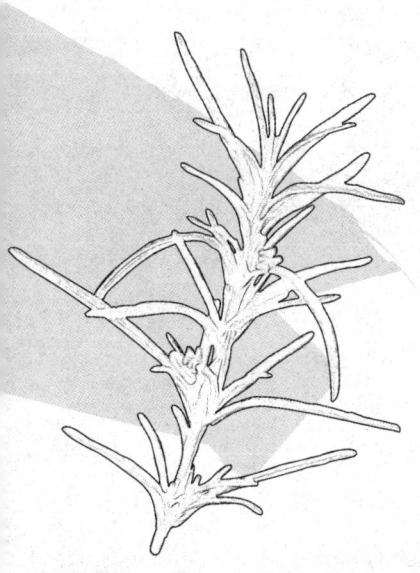

Rosemary

by Edna St. Vincent Millay

For the sake of some things

That be now no more

I will strew rushes

On my chamber-floor,

I will plant bergamot

At my kitchen-door.

For the sake of dim things

That were once so plain

I will set a barrel

Out to catch the rain,

I will hang an iron pot

On an iron crane.

Many things be dead and gone

That were brave and gay;

For the sake of these things

I will learn to say,

"An it please you, gentle sirs,"

"Alack!" and "Well-a-day!"

迷迭香

[美国]埃德娜·圣·文森特·米莱

为了某些如今
已不复存在的东西,
我要把灯芯草
撒上卧室的地板,
我要把佛手柑
种在厨房的门前。

为了某些曾经清楚明朗、
而今却模糊渺茫的东西,
我要放一只水桶
在外面承接雨浆,
我要架一口铁锅
挂在铁吊车之上。

很多东西　现在已湮灭消亡
曾经也勇敢无畏　欢畅昂扬;
为了这些东西
我要学着去说:
"依照您心意,先生们"
"哎呀!"以及"今天不错!"

To Rosemary

by Stephen Vincent Benet

If you were gone afar,

And lost the pattern

Of all your delightful ways,

And the web undone,

How would one make you anew,

From what dew and flowers,

What burning and mingled atoms,

Under the sun?

Not from too-satin roses,

Or those rare blossoms,

Orchids, scentless and precious

As precious stone.

But out of lemon-verbena,

Rose-geranium,

These alone.

Not with running horses,

Or Spanish cannon,

Organs, voiced like a lion,

Clamor and speed.

But perhaps with old music-boxes,

Young, tawny kittens,

Wild-strawberry-seed.

Even so, it were more

Than a god could compass

To fashion the body merely,

The lovely shroud.

But then—ah, how to recapture

That evanescence,

The fire that cried in pure crystal

Out of its cloud!

致迷迭香

[美国] 史蒂芬·文森特·贝内特

如果你身在远方,

失去了所有

讨人喜欢的方法模样,

错综之网也失败收场,

太阳之下,

什么才能让你重获新生,

需要怎样的露珠、花朵,

怎样燃烧和交混的微粒?

不是娇艳如丝缎的玫瑰,

或无香而珍贵的

宝石一般的兰花,

不是那些珍奇的花卉。

而只需柠檬马鞭草,

香叶天竺葵,

这些寂寂无名之辈。

不是奔驰的骏马,

也不是西班牙加农炮，

或声如狮吼的管风琴，

那些喧嚣与迅疾。

而或许只需旧音乐盒，

年幼的茶色猫咪，

或野草莓的种子。

即使如此，仅仅为身体

罩上漂亮的长袍，

就已经超出

神明的筹谋。

但那时——啊，如何重温

那份瞬息幻灭，

当火焰穿透云影

在纯净的水晶中呐喊！

Rosemary

by Marianne Moore

Beauty and Beauty's son and rosemary—
Venus and Love, her son, to speak plainly—
born of the sea supposedly,
at Christmas each, in company,
braids a garland of festivity.
Not always rosemary—

since the flight to Egypt, blooming indifferently.
With lancelike leaf, green but silver underneath,
its flowers—white originally—
turned blue. The herb of memory,
imitating the blue robe of Mary,
is not too legendary

to flower both as symbol and as pungency.
Springing from stones beside the sea,
the height of Christ when he was thirty-three,

it feeds on dew and to the bee

"hath a dumb language"; is in reality

a kind of Christmas tree.

迷迭香

[美国] 玛丽安·摩尔

美、美之子,与迷迭香——
维纳斯和爱神,她的儿子,简单地讲——
据传诞生于海上,
在每个圣诞节相伴,
编织欢庆的花环。
不总是迷迭香——

自从逃往埃及,它冷漠绽放。
长矛状的绿叶,背面泛着银光,
它的花朵——初生是白色——
后又变蓝。记忆之香草,
仿效圣母玛利亚的蓝色长袍,
这不算太过传奇。

对于这既作象征又是辛香料的花朵。
从海边的砾石间冒出,
生长到耶稣三十三岁受难时的高度,

它啜饮露珠,对于蜜蜂,

它"拥有无声的语言";它事实上
是一种圣诞树。

Rosemary

by Ernest McGaffey

Rosemary for remembrance—may this be
A leaf where treasured happiness is sealed
Unknown to others; which to us will yield
(Our memory the magic opening key)
A fragrant scent of the lost days set free
A music to our listening ears revealed;
As a rough shell, that sometimes holds concealed
The mystic murmurous secret of the sea.

For something to the written line belongs
Beyond the word that's uttered; through the pen
This verse, mayhap, shall come to live again
And take its place among remembered songs;
When you and I, and all our love and trust
Are blended into long-forgotten dust.

迷迭香

[美国] 欧内斯特·麦加菲

为作纪念的迷迭香——愿这是

一枚封印了珍贵幸福的叶片

不为外人所见;它为我们带来

(我们的回忆是把钥匙,具有开启的魔力)

一阵逝去岁月静静释放的芬芳

一支向聆听的耳默默倾诉的乐章;

如同一扇粗糙的贝壳,有时

会把海洋玄妙低语的秘密隐藏。

因为有些东西属于书写的诗行

而超出言语能讲;经由笔端

这诗行或许会再次浮现

作为歌谣被人们传唱;

当你,我,我们所有的爱与信任

全都融入久已遗忘的尘土。

Others
其他

The Easter Flower

by Claude McKay

Far from this foreign Easter damp and chilly
My soul steals to a pear-shaped plot of ground,
Where gleamed the lilac-tinted Easter lily
Soft-scented in the air for yards around;

Alone, without a hint of guardian leaf!
Just like a fragile bell of silver rime,
It burst the tomb for freedom sweet and brief
In the young pregnant year at Eastertime;

And many thought it was a sacred sign,
And some called it the resurrection flower;
And I, a pagan, worshiped at its shrine,
Yielding my heart unto its perfumed power.

复活节之花

[美国] 克劳德·麦凯

远离这异国复活节的潮湿与寒意
我的灵魂偷渡到一块梨形土地，
那里闪现着丁香紫色的复活节百合
四围的咫尺之地弥漫着轻柔的香气；

独立枝头，无一丝叶片相守！
像一只纤巧易碎的银霜钟铃，
它为甜蜜而短暂的自由冲破墓穴
在复活节那年轻且孕育的岁月；

很多人将它视作神圣的标志，
有人把它称为复活之花朵；
而我，一个异教徒，拜倒于它的神龛之处，
我的心，被它弥散芳香的力量折服。

Wind and Window Flower

by Robert Frost

Lovers, forget your love,

And list to the love of these,

She a window flower,

And he a winter breeze.

When the frosty window veil

Was melted down at noon,

And the caged yellow bird

Hung over her in tune,

He marked her through the pane,

He could not help but mark,

And only passed her by,

To come again at dark.

He was a winter wind,

Concerned with ice and snow,

Dead weeds and unmated birds,

And little of love could know.

But he sighed upon the sill,
He gave the sash a shake,
As witness all within
Who lay that night awake.

Perchance he half prevailed
To win her for the flight
From the firelit looking-glass
And warm stove-window light.

But the flower leaned aside
And thought of naught to say,
And morning found the breeze
A hundred miles away.

风与窗花

[美国] 罗伯特·弗罗斯特

恋人们,忘记你的爱,

把这一对的爱情倾听,

她是一枝窗上的花朵,

他是一阵冬日的轻风。

当窗户那霜结的面纱

在正午时分消融流淌,

笼中的黄色小鸟

在她的头顶婉转啼唱。

他透过窗棂留意到她,

便忍不住注目凝睐,

他只从她身旁吹过,

入夜后又再度归来。

他是冬日的一阵风,

只关心冷雪寒冰,

枯死的野草和落单的鸟,

对于爱情一无知晓。

可是他在窗台上喟叹,
还把那窗格摇撼,
像是要将窗内看遍,
看看是谁整夜不眠。

或许他已成功过半,
快要赢得她的芳心顾盼,
逃离火光闪耀的玻璃镜面
和温暖炉窗映照的光线。

但那花儿斜倚一旁,
想不出什么话儿来讲,
待到黎明再次到来,
轻风已远在百里之外。

Rose Pogonias

by Robert Frost

A SATURATED meadow,
Sun-shaped and jewel-small,
A circle scarcely wider
Than the trees around were tall;
Where winds were quite excluded,
And the air was stifling sweet
With the breath of many flowers, —
A temple of the heat.

There we bowed us in the burning,
As the sun's right worship is,
To pick where none could miss them
A thousand orchises;
For though the grass was scattered,
yet every second spear
Seemed tipped with wings of color,
That tinged the atmosphere.

We raised a simple prayer

Before we left the spot,

That in the general mowing

That place might be forgot;

Or if not all is favored,

Obtain such grace of hours,

That none should mow the grass there

While so confused with flowers.

玫瑰朱兰

[美国] 罗伯特·弗罗斯特

一片青翠欲滴的草地,

形状如太阳,大小似珠宝,

这一圈地块的宽幅

比周围的树丛高不了多少;

风儿吹不进此地,

空气甜美到令人窒息,

满溢着繁花的浓郁呼吸——

一座热力的庙宇。

我们在那炙烤中弯腰,

像膜拜灿阳的灼烧,

采摘一千朵兰花

那无人能错过的妖娆;

尽管草地疏落凌乱,

但每一截枝叶的顶端

似乎都被彩翼轻触点染,

气氛让人兴奋得震颤。

在离开此地之前
让我们简单做个祷告,
当人们大规模割草时
能够把这里忘掉;
若不能受此偏爱照拂,
也能够得到片刻眷顾,
当花朵与草杂生混淆
没人应该在那割草。

Blue Squills

by Sara Teasdale

How many million Aprils came
Before I ever knew
How white a cherry bough could be,
A bed of squills, how blue!

And many a dancing April
When life is done with me,
Will lift the blue flame of the flower
And the white flame of the tree.

Oh burn me with your beauty then,
Oh hurt me, tree and flower,
Lest in the end death try to take
Even this glistening hour.

O shaken flowers, O shimmering trees,
O sunlit white and blue,
Wound me, that I, through endless sleep,
May bear the scar of you.

蓝铃花

[美国] 萨拉·提斯黛尔

多少次四月来到
我还未察觉知晓,
樱桃的粗枝多么洁白,
这方蓝铃花,如此湛蓝!

多少飘扬舞动的四月,
当生命已与我关系断绝,
将花朵的蓝色火焰
和树木的白焰高举不灭。

哦,用你的美丽灼伤我吧,
伤害我吧,这树和花,
以免最后 死亡想要夺去
这闪闪发光的时节。

花儿随风摇曳,树木微光闪烁,
阳光映照的这白与蓝色,
伤害我吧,让我,在无尽的沉睡中
还能感受到你的伤痕之痛。

As If Some Little Arctic Flower

by Emily Dickinson

As if some little Arctic flower

Upon the polar hem—

Went wandering down the Latitudes

Until it puzzled came

To continents of summer—

To firmaments of sun—

To strange, bright crowds of flowers—

And birds, of foreign tongue!

I say, As if this little flower

To Eden, wandered in—

What then? Why nothing,

Only, your inference therefrom!

如同一朵北极的小花

[美国] 艾米莉·狄金森

如同一朵北极的小花

生长于极地边缘——

沿着纬度漫游南下

直到茫然抵达

夏季炎炎的大陆——

烈日当空的苍穹——

花丛陌生而鲜艳——

禽鸟操着异域方言!

我是说,仿佛这小小的花朵

信步游荡,进入了伊甸园——

之后如何?什么也没有,

只有你由此产生的推测!

Ah! Sun-Flower

by William Blake

Ah Sun-flower! weary of time,

Who countest the steps of the Sun;

Seeking after that sweet golden clime

Where the travellers journey is done.

Where the Youth pined away with desire,

And the pale Virgin shrouded in snow:

Arise from their graves and aspire,

Where my Sun-flower wishes to go.

啊,向阳花

[英国]威廉·布莱克

啊,向阳花!厌倦了时间的流逝,

你计数太阳的脚步;

追随甜蜜如金的地域风土

那里是游子羁旅的归宿。

因渴望而憔悴消陨的少年,

积雪裹尸掩埋的苍白处女:

在那里 从坟墓中起身向往,

我的向阳花想去的地方。

Flowers

by Thomas Hood

I will not have the mad Clytie,

Whose head is turned by the sun;

The tulip is a courtly queen,

Whom, therefore, I will shun;

The cowslip is a country wench,

The violet is a nun—

But I will woo the dainty rose,

The queen of everyone.

The pea is but a wanton witch,

In too much haste to wed,

And clasps her rings on every hand

The wolfsbane I should dread—

Nor will I dreary rosemary

That always mourns the dead—

But I will woo the dainty rose,

With her cheeks of tender red.

The lily is all in white, like a saint,

And so is no mate for me—

And the daisy's cheek is tipped with blush,

She is of such low degree;

Jasmine is sweet, and has many loves,

And the broom's betrothed to the bee—

But I will plight with the dainty rose,

For fairest of all is she.

花

[英国]托马斯·胡德

我不要那发疯的克丽泰,
她只会随太阳转动脑袋;
郁金香有女王的典雅威严,
正因如此,我回避觐见;
莲馨花凡俗村姑一介,
紫罗兰却已遁入空门;
但我会追求娇艳的玫瑰,
所有人心目中的女神。

豌豆花只是个浪荡女巫,
急不可待想要出嫁,
附子草也让我害怕,
用戒指把每只手紧抓——
也不要晦气沉闷的迷迭香,
她总在哀悼死去的亡魂——
但我会追求娇艳的玫瑰,
她嫩红的脸颊明丽可人。

百合一身纯白,像位圣女,

因此不是适合我的伴侣——

雏菊的面腮红霞翩飞,

她的地位卑贱低微;

茉莉甜美,可情人众多,

金雀花已与蜜蜂订立婚约——

而我要向娇艳的玫瑰山盟海誓,

因为她是世间最美的女子。

注:Clytie(克丽泰),希腊神话中因苦恋太阳神阿波罗而化身为向日葵花的女神。

Pear Tree

by Hilda Doolittle

Silver dust

lifted from the earth,

higher than my arms reach,

you have mounted.

O silver,

higher than my arms reach

you front us with great mass;

no flower ever opened

so staunch a white leaf,

no flower ever parted silver

from such rare silver;

O white pear,

your flower-tufts,

thick on the branch,

bring summer and ripe fruits

in their purple hearts.

梨树

[美国] 希尔达·杜利特尔

银白的尘雾

自大地升起;

你攀升的高度,

超出我手臂所及。

哦,银白

高于我手臂所及,

你面朝我们　纷繁盛开。

没有别的花朵

能绽放如此坚挺的洁白叶瓣,

没有别的花朵

能从如此罕见的银白中提纯银白;

哦,洁白的梨花,

你的簇簇花团,

在枝上茂密开放。

把夏日和成熟的果实

纳入它们紫色的花心。